Dear Parent:
Your child's love of reading starts here!

Every child learns to read in a different way and at his or her own speed. Some go back and forth between reading levels and read favorite books again and again. Others read through each level in order. You can help your young reader improve and become more confident by encouraging his or her own interests and abilities. From books your child reads with you to the first books he or she reads alone, there are I Can Read Books for every stage of reading:

SHARED READING
Basic language, word repetition, and whimsical illustrations, ideal for sharing with your emergent reader

BEGINNING READING
Short sentences, familiar words, and simple concepts for children eager to read on their own

READING WITH HELP
Engaging stories, longer sentences, and language play for developing readers

READING ALONE
Complex plots, challenging vocabulary, and high-interest topics for the independent reader

ADVANCED READING
Short paragraphs, chapters, and exciting themes for the perfect bridge to chapter books

I Can Read Books have introduced children to the joy of reading since 1957. Featuring award-winning authors and illustrators and a fabulous cast of beloved characters, I Can Read Books set the standard for beginning readers.

A lifetime of discovery begins with the magical words **"I Can Read!"**

Visit www.icanread.com for information
on enriching your child's reading experience.

For Jonathan Brandt,
a baker of renown
—J.O'C.

For delicious,
delectable, divine Zoe
—R.P.G.

For Diane, whose incredible
cupcakes inspire innumerable
multisyllabic superlatives—
aka fancy words!
—T.E.

I Can Read Book® is a trademark of HarperCollins Publishers.

Library of Congress Cataloging-in-Publication Data
O'Connor, Jane.
    Fancy Nancy and the delectable cupcakes / by Jane O'Connor ; cover illustration by Robin Preiss Glasser ; interior illustrations by Ted Enik. — 1st ed.
        p.   cm. — (Fancy Nancy) (I can read! Level 1)
    Summary: Nancy's failure to pay attention gets her into trouble when she bakes cupcakes for the school bake sale.
    ISBN 978-0-06-188269-2 (trade bdg.) — ISBN 978-0-06-188268-5 (pbk. bdg.)
    [1. Baking—Fiction. 2. Listening—Fiction. 3. Vocabulary—Fiction.] I. Preiss Glasser, Robin. II. Enik, Ted, ill. III. Title.
PZ7.O222Fac 2010   2009030928
[E]—dc22   CIP
                                                               AC

14 15 16 17 18 LP/WOR 10 9 8 7 6 5 4
❖
First Edition

I Can Read!™

BEGINNING READING 1

Fancy NANCY and the Delectable Cupcakes

by Jane O'Connor

cover illustration by Robin Preiss Glasser

interior illustrations by Ted Enik

HARPER

An Imprint of HarperCollinsPublishers

I adore school.

(Adore means to really,

really like something.)

But today I can't wait to go home.

I am going to bake cupcakes—

fancy cupcakes.

"Nancy, did you hear
what I just said?" Ms. Glass asks.
I shake my head.
"I will repeat it," Ms. Glass says.
(Repeat is fancy for saying
something over again.)
"There is no recess tomorrow
because of the bake sale."
The bake sale is to raise money
for library books.

Before I leave,

I go over to Ms. Glass.

"I am sorry.

I wasn't being a good listener."

Ms. Glass smiles.

"I know you are trying to improve."

(Improve is fancy for

getting better at something.)

I hug Ms. Glass.

I adore her. Really I do.

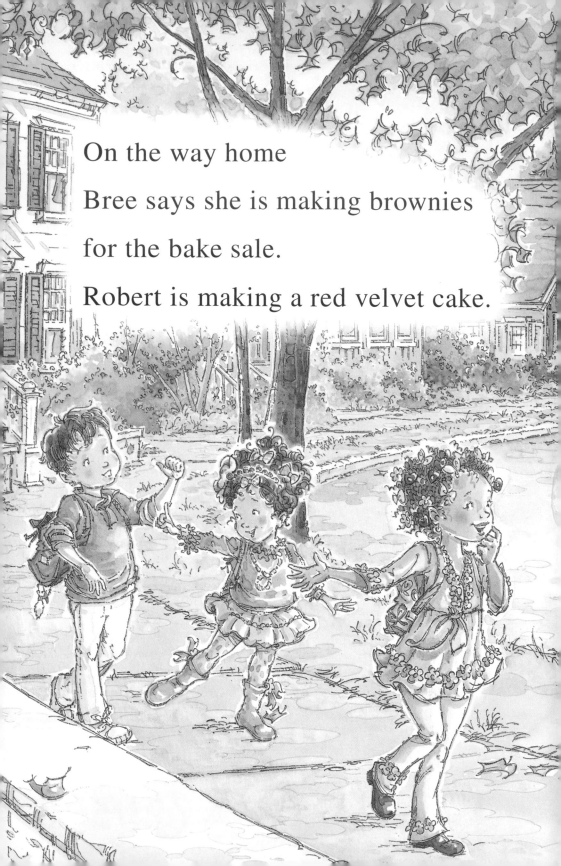

On the way home
Bree says she is making brownies
for the bake sale.
Robert is making a red velvet cake.

It is not really made with velvet.

(That is a very fancy kind of cloth.)

But the inside is all red.

"I will definitely buy a piece,"

I tell him.

At the market, my mom buys
eggs and milk,
flour and sugar,
and butter.

"Don't forget sprinkles and candy,"
I tell her.
It's lucky I am here or we would
end up with plain cupcakes!

I want to start baking right away.

I listen carefully to my mother.

Ms. Glass would be very proud.

I put all the right stuff in the batter.

I pour the batter into the cupcake pan.

My sister is not such a good listener.

My mom tells her three times

to keep her fingers out of the batter.

The cupcakes come out of the oven.

Ooh la la! What a lovely aroma!

(Aroma is fancy for smell.)

When they cool off we put on

frosting and sprinkles and candy.

16

I want to show Mrs. DeVine my cupcakes.

My mom says, "Come back soon.

And be sure to leave the cupcakes

where Frenchy can't get them."

I am already out the door.

Mrs. DeVine buys a cupcake.

She says it is delectable.

(That is fancy for yummy.)

I come home and call Bree.

We make a deal.

I will buy two of her brownies.

She will buy two of my cupcakes.

I hope I sell all of them.

A minute later I hang up.

Then I see Frenchy's face.

Frosting is all over her mouth!

Oh no!

The cupcakes are a mess.

"Nancy, didn't you listen?"

my mom asks.

"I said to leave them in a safe place."

23

"It is all my fault.

I wasn't listening,"

I tell my mom.

Just then my dad comes home.

I tell him what happened.

"Now I don't have cupcakes

for the bake sale."

"Cupcakes?" my dad says.

"You baked cupcakes already?"

Then he holds out a big bag.

In it is all the stuff for cupcakes.

"I told you I would buy everything,"

both my parents say at the same time.

Then they start laughing.

I laugh too.

Nobody in my family is a good listener!

After dinner

we bake cupcakes all over again.

I am exhausted.

(That's fancy for very tired.)

My dad says,

"Nancy, please get ready for bed."

Guess what?

For once, he doesn't have to

repeat himself!

The bake sale is a big success.

My cupcakes are all gone.

"Oh!" I say to my mom.

"I didn't even get to taste one."

"Look!" my mom says.

She saved one for me.

I taste it.

Mmm. Totally delectable.

Fancy Nancy's Fancy Words

These are the fancy words in this book:

Adore—to really, really like something

Aroma—a smell

Delectable—yummy

Exhausted—very tired

Improve—to get better at something

Repeat—to say something over again

Velvet—a very fancy kind of cloth